THE FAILED HERO

And Other Short Stories

THE FAILED HERO

And Other Short Stories

Written by Lilah Lyons

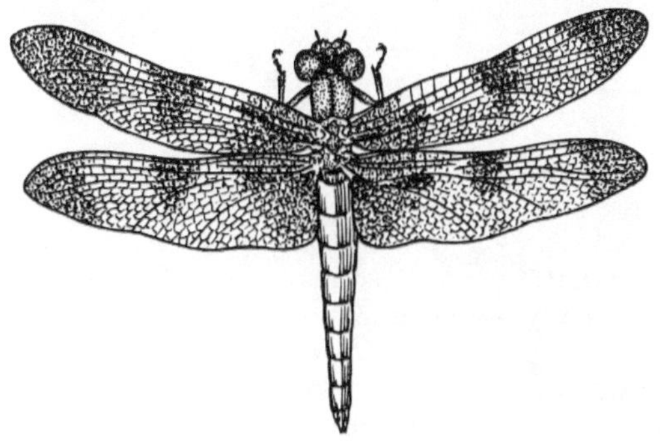

ISBN 9798218421038
Copyright © 2024 by Lilah Lyons

This novel is entirely a work of fiction. The names, characters and incidents portrayed in it are the work of the author's imagination. Any resemblance to actual persons, living or dead, events or localities is entirely coincidental.

Edited by Lottie Hayes-Clemens

Cover design by Lilah Lyons. Illustrations and fonts taken from Canva.

Table of Contents

- - - Dedication - - -

Everything I do is for You
My life is Your altar

"It seems the way to find some things is to
lose yourself."

— George MacDonald

Many Thanks

I want to take a moment and thank all the wonderful people who made this book possible. First, my parents, who encouraged me every step of the way. To my brother, Gavin, who gave me something to strive for; to Robin Lyons, who helped me financially; and to Edmund Goforth, who provided much needed feedback. I would also like to thank Mattie Taylor for dealing with my many complaints and my proofreader and editor, Lottie, for tidying up my first draft.

Lastly, I would like to thank you, dear reader, for picking up this obscure little book and deciding it would be worth your while to read it.

PART ONE
SHORT STORIES

These tales though short each hold some desire
Of burning breath and consuming fire

However they find you, let them impart
The wishes of my secret heart

But, moreover, let them be
More use to you than they are for me

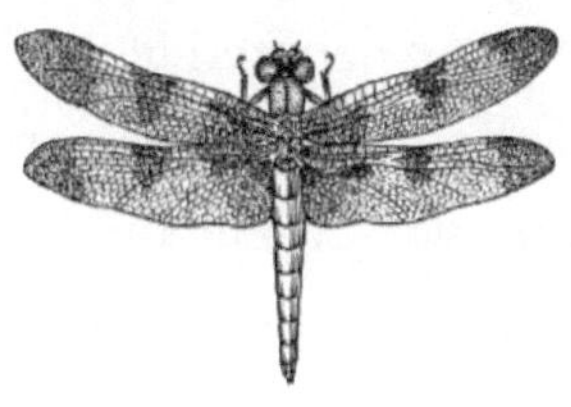

How the Old Man Died

he day the old man died started like any other. He woke before dawn and was out of bed by seven, seating himself at his table for breakfast by seven-thirty. After eating his toast and eggs, and downing a handful of bitter-tasting pills, he put on his jacket and left for work.

He was a crotchety, bent old fellow, whose dislikes far surpassed his likes. His home was joined to his neighbors by a thin wall, which did little to block the noise of their four rowdy children. To avoid their commotion, he spent as little time as he could at home, and made himself so frightening that they never bothered him.

People cleared the sidewalk as he passed, leaving him alone without as much as a friendly nod. It is a strange thing when neighbors cease to be neighborly. It makes one wonder which came first: the sullenness of one or the shyness of the other.

As the old man walked down the street, he frowned at a little boy riding his bike across the pavement. As soon as the child noticed him he peddled away rather quickly, frightened by the old man's cross expression. The man grunted and continued shuffling down the sidewalk. He was feeling weaker than usual today and had a tingling sensation in his shoulder.

When he arrived at work it was starting to drizzle. The dull pat-pattering of the water droned monotonously in the already drab atmosphere as he opened shop. He worked as a cashier for the town's general store, but they seldom had customers.

Toys, Goods, and Clothing! read the sign outside. *Andy's General Store for All Your General Needs.*

No one would be stopping by today. The rain started coming down harder, banging on the thin metal roof like children banging on pots and pans.

At least that's what the old man thought when he heard it. He lazily looked out the window and thought of his annoying neighbors. Why did children have to be so loud? He certainly never yelled when he wanted something, and he never decided to peek through the holes in anyone's fence. Thinking it over, he decided that he was the model of neighborly goodness. Never treading in *their* flowerbeds or upsetting *their* sleep. How lucky they were to have such a saint living next door!

As he was thinking, he saw a blue jacket appear in the street. It was a woman, or rather, a girl, walking in the rain without an umbrella. She was smiling up at the graying sky and didn't seem at all alarmed at getting wet. Something about her countenance made the old man stiffen. *What a fool,* he thought.

She saw him looking at her from inside the shop and came in.

"Hello!" she smiled, as she pushed the door open, the brass doorbell jingling merrily at her entrance.

"Mornin'," grunted the old man.

"What a nice shop! Do you sell tins of ginger snaps?"

"Yes, ma'am. Near the back. Right of the pickles."

"Thanks," she said and disappeared down one of the aisles, leaving a watery trail of footsteps behind her. "Isn't the weather beautiful today?" she called out across the store. The old man just ignored her.

She came back with two tins of ginger snaps, a jar of pickles, and a packet of wildflower seeds. "Isn't the rain nice?" she asked again.

"It's wet," the old man grumbled and started tallying up her purchase.

"I really can't think why more people aren't out today. I was walking through the woods this morning when the rain came and I nearly leaped for joy. Oh, you should have seen it! It was beautiful!" The girl's mind seemed to drift far away, like she was still gazing at the rain-bathed woods, staring at the sunlight glinting on each quiet raindrop.

She must be insane, thought the man. *It's just rain. Nobody likes the rain.*

"It rains a lot this time of year," he said. "Better get used to it. No use in calling the commonplace beautiful. It isn't."

"But that's what makes it even lovelier," she mused. "When the rain comes, it's like the coming of an old friend. And each raindrop that falls on my face is like a kiss. Oh, it's so good to be alive!"

The man shrugged.

"That will be sixteen dollars and twenty-five cents."

"Oh, right. Here you go." She handed him a twenty-dollar bill. "Keep the change." She took her items and turned to leave.

"We sell umbrellas," the old man said quickly as the girl started out the door. She turned around and looked at him quizzically.

"No, thank you. Why would I want one of those?"

Just as I thought, said the old man to himself. *She's a lunatic.*

He took his lunch break about an hour later and washed down some more pills with flat soda. His right shoulder was still tingling and he reached over to rub the sensation out.

"Stars," he said aloud. "It just keeps getting worse."

As the day continued, the feeling spread across his shoulder and throughout his arm. It made it impossible to mop the floor or stack the boxes he needed to organize. Even the simple task of taking inventory left him a little breathless. When half his face went numb, he started to panic. He needed to call someone. He had learned what number to call for things like this. What number was it? He couldn't remember. Was it 811? 199?

The man opened his small flip phone and speed-dialed his doctor. The regular office recording began to play.

"This is Milton Family Hospital, if you are inquiring on the status of a patient please dial one. If you need to speak with a doctor in the children's ward, please dial two…"

"I think I'm having a stroke," he slurred into the phone. His head hurt. It felt like someone was hammering behind his eyes.

"If you are experiencing a medical emergency," the recording went on. "Please hang up and dial 911…"

He fumbled with his phone and dialed the number. His vision was blurring.

"911, what is your emergency?"

"I think I'm having a stroke," he mumbled. His lips didn't want to work.

"Alright, sir, we will send someone over. Stay calm. Sit down, sir, and keep us on the line. This is the general store, yes?"

"Uh-huh," he said, easing himself onto the floor. His hands were shaking uncontrollably, he couldn't hold the phone anymore. The person on the line was trying to talk to him, trying to keep him from panicking, but the old man wasn't listening. Everything hurt and nothing made sense.

Think, think, think, he told himself. *Think? Think what?* His brain wasn't working anymore. All he could concentrate on was the rain humming on the roof. *Just breathe*, he thought, *breathe.*

It took a full twenty minutes for the ambulance to arrive. The workers loaded him into a stretcher and kept asking him questions.

"Do you have a wife?" they asked. "Do you have a family? Any friends we should contact?"

"No, no, no," he mumbled. No, he didn't have anyone, not anymore. Not even a dog to keep him company.

They took him to the hospital, checked his vitals, and did a scan. A doctor came in and gave him some medicine. It made him feel like throwing up, or perhaps that was just the stroke.

"We will keep you here for a few days, depending on how you are doing," informed the doctor. She was a youngish-looking woman wearing blue scrubs. It made him think of the girl in the blue coat.

"Will I die?" he asked.

She pursed her lips. "We'll just have to wait it out."

"Will I die?" he asked again, his voice cracking this time.

"Some people survive strokes, sir. Others don't. The best thing to do is just rest. I'll have a nurse check on you in a bit."

"What ward?"

The doctor seemed to understand his question.

"You're in ICU," she whispered. "Near the critical patients. Get some rest, sir. You need all your strength." Then she left him alone.

He lay there groggily in the hospital bed, feeling shaky and afraid. *I am dying*, he realized, despite what the doctor had said. *I am actually dying and will be dead in just a moment. Where have the years gone?*

He wondered if his life would flash before his eyes. What would there be to see? Who would remember him when he was gone? He had nobody, nothing!

He lay there in the hospital bed, feeling sad and miserable, when something the girl in the blue coat said came back to him.

Oh, it's so good to be alive!

A sparrow was sitting on the ledge of the open hospital window. It was looking at him curiously with small black eyes. There was nothing special about it, nothing wonderful. In fact, it was a rather plain little thing. But to the old man, it was the most beautiful creature he had ever seen.

"Little bird," he said through parched lips. "Little bird. I'm dying. I'm afraid to die."

The bird hopped along the window ledge.

"Tell them that life is good. Tell them 'enjoy simple things,' because the end comes soon."

The monitor he was hooked up to started beeping wildly. The medicine had not prevented a second stroke. The world seemed to spin and reel about the old man, all color and noise and the loud beep beep beep of the monitor growing louder as his heart sputtered like an old engine. His thoughts didn't make sense, and no amount of air could fill his lungs. He tried to sit up and call for the nurse, but the only sound he could make was a quiet gurgling like a stream filled with rainwater. Through all his incoherent babble, one sentence was still able to form in his mind. *This is my end*, he thought, trying not to cry, *have courage.*

He felt a film steal over his eyes, and with that, cold death took his life.

The bird flew away to a nearby tree where it fluffed its feathers and started singing, overjoyed at the sun parting the rain clouds.

"What a lovely bird," said a man to his wife as they passed by.

"Yes, what a beautiful song," returned his wife, nodding her head in agreement. "I wish I knew what it was singing about."

They stopped for a moment, admiring the drab little bird that sang so blithely.

"Oh, don't be silly," said their daughter, eager to be done with the walk. "It's just a bird. It's not singing about anything."

A Lily Garden

he stood on a square plinth in the exact center of the pond and had for a long while, her eyes growing green with moss and feet bathed in the scent of water lilies. She watched everything in her walled garden with great interest, pondering silently the willow tree and thrush nest hidden in the shrubbery.

As winter blew over her waters, making ripples across its glassy surface, a new visitor came. A dark-faced man stared at her in the winter-dead garden. He breathed on his hands to warm them, then walked around the overwintered flowerbeds, stopping to look at the statue every few minutes. Few people had watched her with such intensity before, and it perplexed her.

Once, a child had pointed at her and cried "Mother! Mother!" which caused her father to scoop her up and press her to his chest. He cried into his daughter's hair as he did, whispering words of comfort to the grieving girl, but never had the statue been an object of interest for more than a moment or so. The man who now watched her had come round the garden three times and at present stood at the pond's bank. His eyes were sad and downcast. After another look, he sighed and moved on.

But the man was back the next day with a book, and the next, paper and charcoal. He began to draw the statue, sitting on a bench nearby. She eyed him with uncertainty at first, ever smiling but unsure of his company. Then she blushed softly when she realized what he was doing. The statue was shy about getting her picture drawn, but secretly very pleased. The man, too, seemed happier than he had been. He came nearly every day, and the statue found herself looking forward to his company. It was not long before she wished her mute lips could speak, especially when he began speaking to her.

"I wonder how many fish are in that little pond of yours," he asked as the days grew warmer. He laughed at himself for speaking to the stone girl but did so anyway. "It seems like more are hatching by the day. Why look! There is a cloud of little ones."

The statute wanted to reply; "Yes! And the lilies are waking as well, and the tulips by the bank." But she was only able to smile.

"You are very lovely," he said to her. "I like this garden because you are in it. I was lonely last winter, but now you keep me company." Then he began to whistle like a boy, and walk about her garden as usual. The statue's heart beat very fast and she wanted to leap from her plinth and walk alongside him, pointing out each of her garden's secrets, which only many years of patient watching had shown her. Instead, she only gazed at the man as he picked up smooth pebbles and slipped them into his coat pocket.

But then the man was gone for nearly a month and the statue could no longer content herself with the comings and goings of summer. She would strain her ear to hear the sound of boots crunching gravel on the path, or the boyish whistling the man had taken up, but all she ever heard was the chattering of cicadas and the droning lullaby of bees flying from lily to lily.

Other people came into her walls, sure. Young couples and families with children. The sunshine was bringing them out of their homes and into the city parks. But they only made her feel lonelier. It was odd, she thought, to feel so solitary when there were so many people around her. When she did see the man again, he was changed.

He laughed with the woman next to him and took her around the garden.

"What did you do while I was away?" she asked.

"Nothing much," he said honestly. "I mostly just wandered and moped. I went to this garden a lot though. I like that little sculpture over there. She looks a bit like you." And the man pointed at the statue admiringly. "I have half a mind to make a clay copy. I did some sketches last February."

The woman looked up at the man. "You should switch schools," she said. "Then we won't have to spend so much time apart."

"It's you that lives far away!" he laughed.

The woman shrugged. "I don't like the city. You should come study art in the countryside. It's quiet there. Pretty. I often take walks by the river and collect ferns and moss. There's plenty to paint out there."

"There's also plenty to paint in the city. And some good universities for your botany."

"How can I study botany when there are no plants to study?" she asked. "Though–" she tilted her head. "This place is nice. All the flowers." The man and woman smiled at one another.

The statue looked at them blankly from the center of the pond. She felt like a trapped bird wanting to fly from its perch, but could not move an inch from where she stood. A raindrop fell on the pond's glassy surface and disturbed a snail crawling across the edge of a lily pad.

"A storm's coming," said the man. "Want to wait it out at my house?"

More drops fell, and the man and woman left. The garden became sodden with mud and puddles. Rain fell upon the statue and ran down her cheeks like rivulets of tears. She felt as if a large crack started in her chest and fragmented her stone. She stared at the water lilies below with a sad smile plastered on her face. Slowly, she let out a sigh. The thrush hid its head sorrowfully in its wings and the daffodils drooped their long necks, and the wind carried her sigh across the water and left it tangled in the cattails.

THE LOCKET

t was a regular autumn day in Massachusetts. The clouds looked like lambs on a hazy blue hillside, and dry leaves scattered themselves on the forest floor.

A man in a brown plaid suit was walking down a narrow trail with his hands in his pockets. He was a good-looking man of about twenty, with messy dark hair and a cheerful smile.

The angry chattering of two chipmunks resounded in the wood as they scampered up an old grandfather oak. The man looked up at the almost leafless boughs and chuckled to himself. He was in the sort of mood where anything could make him smile. He was bubbling over with joy. He and his fiancée, Emma—beautiful, blue-eyed Emma, he thought wistfully—were to be married in less than a month. He had become so intolerably excited that his roommates had urged him to get out of the house before he drove them mad.

He strolled down the autumn-painted path with no destination in mind. He loved walking, but never went to this park. Emma always told him it was trashy, and that he shouldn't waste his time.

"Really," she had said, nodding her pretty brunette head, "it's nothing but broken glass and old newspapers. The whole area is run-down."

But the man didn't notice any of this as he walked. It was picture perfect, not a blade of grass out of place.

But as the trees' shadows darkened, growing longer as the afternoon turned to evening, the man found himself in a less kept part of the grounds. The gravel path was washed away in a few parts and thistles were growing on its borders. But the trees— that was the strange thing— the trees in this part of the forest were planted in perfectly straight rows. They were tall too, much taller than the rest of the forest. The man looked at them curiously.

"Almost like an orchard," he said aloud.

He walked over to the first tree in the line and put his hand up to the flaking bark. The tree felt so full of life, and the man liked knowing it was alive. He rested his ear on the trunk and thought he could hear the sap flowing in the tree.

"Maple trees," he said and smiled.

I wonder what it's like to lay dormant all winter, thought the man, *dead, really, then come back to life in the spring. I wonder if the trees feel any pain when their leaves fall. Are they just drifting off to sleep or does it really feel like dying?*

The woodland seemed to stretch from infinity to infinity. So far back that curiosity took hold of him. What lay at the end of the trees? The ruins of a farmhouse? Did the trees just go on forever? As he walked through the rows, his steps were muffled by the soft mattress of yellowed grass. The lowest branches had already lost their leaves, but the treetops were fully clothed, filtering out much of the light. The sun was getting still lower in the sky and casting shade, but the man didn't notice the forest growing hazy and dark around him. He was too transfixed by the trees.

"It is so cold," he mumbled absently, never looking back at the path. "It's freezing and very still."

A thick mist clung to the air. The moisture forming water droplets on the branches and dripping onto the man's face. He didn't even stop to wipe them off. His hands were fidgeting nervously with a button on his jacket, and he seemed oblivious of his surroundings. He was drawn to whatever lay past the trees. He was trying to stay calm, telling himself it was just curiosity or the damp air making him feel strange. "I'm just antsy and walking will do me good," he said.

But he was lying to himself and he knew it.

Just as the fog grew thickest, the trees opened up and an old cottage sat in a clearing before him. He nearly ran towards it.

From a few feet away he could smell the damp stones and musty thatched roof. It was very cold here. Very, very cold. Hadn't it been warm earlier?

"Cold, cold. That day was cold. I felt cold," he murmured. Then he shook his head to clear his brain. What was he talking about? This was nonsense. He had never been here before. Still, all he could think about was the cold, how *That February* had been so very cold.

As he walked into the dilapidated building, something shiny caught his eye. Wedged into a crack between two old floorboards was a small piece of metal. The man bent down to inspect it, prying it out of its hiding place with a twig. It was a locket.

As he struggled to open the locket, it felt very warm in his hands, as if someone had just been holding it. The man's hands were shaking as the necklace popped open.

Inside, there was a minuscule picture of a woman. She had long brown hair and eyes of the deepest blue. Whoever painted her picture must have been a true master to convey the depth of her eyes. Below, in small curly script, read:

Emma, 1692.

"Emma," the man said slowly. He seemed to be having trouble saying the name. Something about it was lying heavy on his tongue. "Emmaaaa," he said again. His eyes went wide. "It's Emma!"

Suddenly he felt like he was being pushed through glass, for certainly there was a crack akin to the splintering of a window. The world whirled around him. Clutching his head, he kneeled to keep himself from falling over. The earth seemed to be spinning backward at an alarming rate. The cottage was bending and changing around him. Walls were filling in, shattered windows were fixing themselves, sturdy wood was replacing the rotten floorboards. An oil lamp was thrown onto a table, flowers were stuffing themselves into a vase. A flurry of color and noise flashed past him. Twisting, scratching, running in every direction.

And then, just as it started, it stopped.

The cottage seemed a pleasant place now. A small fire was burning on the hearth and simple furniture adorned the room. It was warm here, cozy, starkly different from the wintery day outside. As the man looked up, his breath was ragged and a bead of sweat trickled down his temple.

"Where…?" he started, but he already knew. He stood up and walked swiftly over to the single-pane window.

And there it was, the bakery, the tanner, the young maple grove. He planted those trees and his father owned the bakery.

"No, no, no." He shook his head. His father was not a baker and he had not planted any trees.

Right? Right.

"I have never been here before," he said.

But he did not believe it.

A Bedtime Story

"Quiet now, children," said a woman one night, as she pulled the covers over her children, their four little beds lining the wall of their room. "Quiet now," said the woman again, as a few giggles escaped the lips of the youngest, and only girl, of the family. "Hush and I will tell you a story."

"Is it a true story?" asked the oldest, a skeptical boy of eight.

"True enough," said their mother, nodding her head as she dimmed the light. "Now listen, and you can judge the truth for yourself.

"Once upon a time…" she began, seating herself on the foot of one of the beds. "Once upon a time there was a poor fermă—"

"What's a fermă?" asked the rosy-cheeked little girl.

"Hey! No 'ruptin' the story!" said one of her older brothers.

"A fermă is like a farm," said their mother patiently, smoothing a curl from her son's brow. "It's what they called farms in faraway places."

"Aren't you from a faraway place, Mother?" asked another one of the boys. Their mother nodded.

"In this fermă," she went on, "there was a little girl who never had enough to eat. This girl was so poor that she could not leave the house in winter. She had no shoes, you see, and the snow would fall thick and white outside. Her toes would get so cold that her mother wrapped them in rags to keep them warm. The little girl knew children whose feet really had frozen, and they walked stiffly because of it."

"Why didn't she ask for some shoes from Santa?" asked the little girl, innocently looking at her mother.

"Santa never came to that poor country, my love," the woman said sadly. "Or perhaps the little girl was not good enough and he skipped over her." She was quiet for a moment, then shook herself and smiled. "What am I saying?" she laughed. "That girl was a very good child. Only, sometimes she wondered why God let her stay so poor. She was always very hungry, and always very cold. If she was bad she would have gotten coal. How she would have loved to get a lump of coal! Coal means fire, and fire means warmth for cold fingers and toes. It is a terrible thing to be cold.

"One day, her father, the farmer of the fermă, decided they must all leave their country. He said they must leave because their country was no longer safe for people like them."

"Why not?" asked the oldest.

The children watched the familiar face of their mother in the dark room, her forehead wrinkling in thought like crumpled paper.

"There were trolls," she said finally. She seemed to like the idea and went with it. "Yes, that's what they were, trolls. They had small, quick black eyes for spying and big warty hands for catching. People started disappearing, so her father said they must go.

"The girl said goodbye to all her favorite haunts in the forest, and led her little goat away to market tearfully. She packed one small suitcase, and away they went. But first, they had to cross a wide ocean. The biggest ocean in the world.

"The ship the girl traveled on was cramped and smelled like rotten fruit. For the first time in her life, the girl was not hungry. She felt too sick to be hungry. Her father told her to stay in sight, because, he said, the ship was a dangerous place for little girls."

"Why?" asked another boy. "Were there dragons on the boat?"

"I think so," said the woman. "There were always frightening and angry-looking people staring at the girl. I think they must have been the dragons.

"They traveled all the way across the sea to a place where the people spoke a different language and wore odd clothes without much color. The little girl was glad to be safe from the trolls and dragons but cried whenever she thought of her old home. Each day she thought of her friends, so far away, and prayed they would be safe from the trolls.

"But soon the little girl learned to love her new country, not quite like her old one, but close. She made new friends, and her father and mother made enough money to buy lots of food. And so the little girl grew rosy and plump on soups and sandwiches and pie. It was delicious! She even got shoes and pranced about all winter.

"All of a sudden, the girl was a young woman and had to help her parents make money. She decided she must go to work. When she was seventeen, she put up her long yellow hair and got a job at a factory."

"What did she make?" asked a child.

"Bottles for magic potions," the woman said matter-of-factly.

"No more 'ruptin!" said the oldest boy, again.

"No fair! Everyone's been doing it!"

"Children!" laughed their mother. "Don't you want to know what happened next?" Four curly blonde heads nodded in unison.

"The girl saved up money, and bit by bit she learned to provide for herself. You couldn't tell her apart from the others who lived in the country now, she dressed and spoke just like them.

"One day she met a handsome man and fell in love. He was poor just like her, but I think he was a prince in disguise. One day they went to a church to be wed. The girl wore a big white dress and didn't feel poor at all.

"And there were flowers everywhere…

"And her father and mother were sitting in the church pews…

"And her friends all cheered as she walked down a long, long, aisle…"

The children were nodding off now. Their mother looked at them sweetly, kissed each one on their brow, and turned to go.

"Mother, are you sure that story is true?" asked one child, sleepily.

But he spoke only to the dark, for his mother had slipped from the room.

HEARTLESS

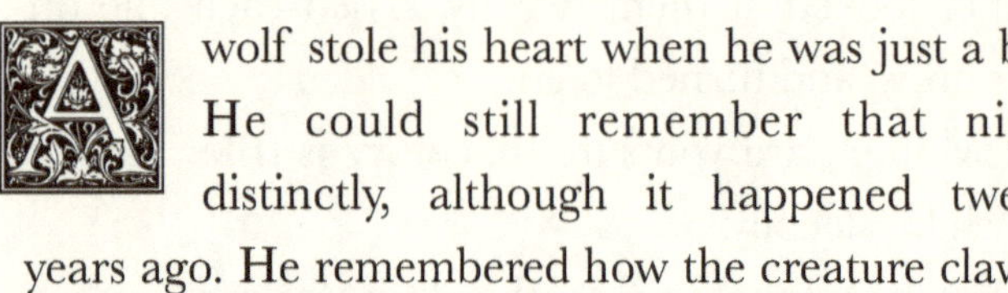

A wolf stole his heart when he was just a boy. He could still remember that night distinctly, although it happened twelve years ago. He remembered how the creature clawed at his young flesh, its hungry jaws eager and snapping.

Max used to live in a grimy little house bordering the woods. The house was actually a mobile home his father had bought when his parents got divorced. He bought it "real cheap," as his father would have said, and felt no need to fix the leaks, cracks, and drafts that blew through that hollow dump.

Each night, Max would lay down into his secondhand bed and wonder why nobody tucked him in. Then, he would rise early for school the next morning and get ready by himself. He would pour a bowl of cereal in the half light of the kitchen then walk a quarter of a mile to the bus stop. As he got older he began to wonder why nobody greeted him when he got home, why nobody attended his school plays, and why it seemed like he had always taken care of himself.

I need a mom, he thought one day as he was making himself dinner. All the other kids had moms, so why didn't he? He supposed that he had probably had one once (his existence wouldn't make much sense otherwise) but she probably left or got tired of taking care of him.

"Hey, Dad," he asked the evening before the wolf came. It was getting late, and Max was already in his pajamas. "Why did mom leave?"

His father was sitting on the stained old recliner in the living room, surrounded by empty beer cans and limply flipping through TV channels. He glanced at his son with a bleary eye.

"What'd you say?"

"How come I don't have a mom?"

"Dunno," responded his father, looking back at the screen.

"Oh… Did she love me?"

His dad shrugged and continued flipping through channels. He found a cop show and stopped.

"Do you love me, Dad?"

Max watched the man's face twist into a frown.

"Dunno."

"But…" Max's lip was quivering. "Dad, you have to love me. I'm your son."

His father opened another can and took a big swig. "I don't gotta do nothin'. Just let me watch my show."

"Daddy!" Max cried.

"Get lost, boy." With a half-hearted toss, his father clumsily threw one of the cans at his son.

Max backed up slowly and ran through the door. His father motioned as though to call out to his son, but hesitated and opened another drink.

Max ran as fast as his ten-year-old legs could carry him and didn't stop running until he was deep in the woods. His bare feet stumbled over rocks hidden deep within the fallen leaves. The tree branches grabbed at him like they wanted to hold him back, as if they were warning him not to go deeper into the woods, but Max was too upset to notice. Soon, he was in an unrecognizable part of the forest and puffing to catch his breath.

Max sat down at the foot of a tree and cried. He kept thinking, *I'm a bad son, I'm a bad son, I'm a bad son. That's why Mom left. That's why Dad doesn't love me. I try to be good, although I don't always get the best grades. I still try. Why can't he see that I try? My father is mean. I don't love him. That's why he doesn't love me. He knows I hate him, so he hates me right back.*

Perhaps the wolf wouldn't have come if Max had uprooted the weeds growing inside him. But there is no use in speculation. Max was only a child, and he didn't know any better. He stayed in the woods the whole night.

That's when the wolf came.

Max heard its soft padding feet circling him and he smelled the stench of its jaws. The smell was centuries old, of wars, and buried secrets, and dark tunnels, and crooked smiles, but Max was too angry to feel any fear.

"What do you want?" he yelled.

"What do I want?" said the wolf. "I don't want anything. The real question is, what do you want?"

"I want to be loved," said Max. He wiped his runny nose on his pajama sleeve. "I want to be a good son."

The wolf laughed, a sound between a whine and a howl. "Silly, innocent boy." The wolf was circling closer and closer now. Max could almost feel its thick gray fur touch his face. "You don't really want love. What you really want, only I can give you."

"What's that?" asked Max.

"You want to be happy," the wolf whispered in his ear. "You don't ever want to be hurt by someone again."

"Yes," Max whispered back. "That's what I want."

Then the wolf leapt upon him.

Bitter, was the only thought in Max's head the next morning. *I am very bitter and I hate my father. I don't care what he thinks anymore.*

Max and his father barely spoke after that night. When Max turned seventeen, he got a job and left home. He saved up, paid his way to college, and never looked back. His father tried to call him once, but Max didn't answer. He just stared at the phone as it rang, feeling nothing.

Twelve years is a long time to be without a heart.

* * *

Max looked out of his office window into the busy street. He liked to watch the people walk to and fro on the pavement and see the cars zoom down the road. The people below never looked up at his dark face haunting the office building. They were too absorbed in their own lives to notice the somber face on the other side of the glass. They wouldn't have seen anything cheerful if they did, just a man with an unsettling countenance, looking down at them like they were nothing but beetles.

Max's desk was situated on the second story of the company's building and was one of the only cubicles with a window. It was reserved for valuable employees, and Max took much pride in the fact that he was considered important enough to occupy it.

This is it, he thought on the day of his promotion. *I'm happy. And I did it all myself, no thanks to anyone else.*

Sure, maybe he hadn't done all the work credited to him, and maybe he had pulled a few strings behind the scenes, but all's well that ends well, right?

"Say, Max," said his coworker, bringing Max back to the present. A tall man with a mustache leaned over the dividing wall of the cubical, twirling the end of his sandy-blonde whiskers. "The wife and I are having a dinner party tonight and I was wondering if you wanted to come. I don't know if you already had plans but…"

The two men were not friends. Max did not have any friends, but his good-natured coworker did not know this. Max smiled at the man and nodded like a dinner party was a great idea. The man was moving up the ranks at work, and Max wanted to come.

"Of course," he said with a grin. "I'd love to stop by."

Max showed up to the party carrying a bottle of wine under his arm. He seldom drank anything alcoholic, even at parties, but Max knew a bottle of wine could do wonders impressing a host.

Time to make a good impression, he thought, smoothing a wrinkle in his button-up. He had long ago realized the quickest way to make a man like you is to make their wife like you. Once you had an advocate inside their home, getting people to trust you at work was simple. He had done many deals this way and made quite a bit of profit.

The door opened and he was greeted by a woman in her mid-thirties. "Come on in!" she said warmly, taking the bottle from Max. "Oh, this wine looks good. Carl is in the living room. Car-al!" she called from the doorstep. "Carl, your friend is here!"

The house was homey and inviting. A few guests were already there, sitting on a low sofa in the living room and eating crackers with cheese. Carl, the man with the sandy mustache, got up from where he sat to greet Max, slapping him on the back like they were brothers.

"Hey, Max! Welcome," Carl said as he shook Max's hand. "Care for a drink?"

"Oh, no thank you," said Max, eyeing the beer can in Carl's other hand. Max never drank beer, leastways, not out of a can.

A little girl appeared in the hallway, dressed in a fuzzy white robe. She was carrying a stuffed rabbit and went over to Carl's wife, tugging at her skirt. Her auburn hair fell in baby ringlets around her shoulders and looked shiny and soft as down.

"Mommy, can I have a snack?" she asked.

"Oh, Anna, what are you doing out of bed?" She turned in Carl's direction. "Dear!"

"Coming," said Carl, as he went over to his daughter. "Just a moment, Max.

"A snack, you said?" Carl cooed, lowering himself onto his haunches so his eyes could meet with his child. The girl nodded eagerly. She couldn't have been more than four.

"How about some cheese?" said her father. Her face broke into a big smile as Carl plucked some off a platter and handed it to her. She shoved it all into her little mouth with delight.

"My favorite!" she said between bites. Then her mother led her away to bed with a kind, but firm; "Now stay put till morning."

"Kids," said Carl, returning to Max. "They are the funniest little things. I love mine to bits."

Max nodded, but inwardly he felt a strange emotion gnawing in his chest. He had never cared for children before, they were so needy, so *irritating*. So why did Max feel like he wouldn't mind having one himself? Not now, of course. He was busy, much too busy for that. But maybe someday. It might be nice to meet a smart young woman, settle down, and have a family of his own.

No, Max told himself. *You came here to get better at business, not to daydream. That life is not for you.*

"How many do you have?" asked Max. He knew he should drop the subject, but reasoned that it would score him more points with his host.

"Just three," said Carl. "But sometimes it feels like they are swinging from the rafters. Lucy, my wife, is actually expecting another one, but she isn't showing just yet." He beamed at his wife across the room, where she had reinstated herself after putting their daughter to bed. She nodded her head to her husband from the midst of a group of friends, winking and smiling at him.

"Congrats," said Max, the gnawing feeling getting stronger.

How strange, he thought, *I've never felt like this before.*

Max soon became the life of the party. He always did. He was good with people. But as he chatted idly about sports and politics and business deals, all he thought about was little Anna calling to her mother. She trusted her parents loved her and would never leave her. It made him feel odd, uncomfortable even. *I don't understand love at all*, he realized.

You don't need love, he felt something whisper to him. The voice was quiet and raspy. It sounded familiar, but Max couldn't quite place where he had heard it. *All love does is hurt you*, it went on. *Love always hurts. Why cause yourself pain? That is all it is. Pain, pain, pain…*

Max pushed the thought out of his head. "You're right," he whispered back, "hearts are heavy. I'm glad I don't have one."

The evening passed as would be expected. Pot roast and salad for dinner, with glasses of the wine Max brought. He was glad when the guests declared it "fantastic" and asked him where he bought it. Even Max himself took a few sips of the stuff, just to quiet his babbling mind. He felt the wine's warmth spread over him like a small fire, dulling his senses and the ache in his chest.

When it was time to leave, Max was glad to go. He opened the door to his car and slid into the driver's seat, putting his key in the ignition. That's when he smelled it.

What is that stench? he wondered as he looked around his car. *It reeks of dog in here!* He turned on his car light and twisted himself to face the backseat. Max's car was usually spotless. He kept it so clean that anyone would have assumed it was brand new.

"What on earth—!" he exclaimed. The entirety of his backseat was covered in coarse black hair. It smelled musty and damp like some wild dog had rolled in something dead and then laid across the seats. A creeping sense of dread ran down Max's spine. *It's nothing,* he told himself as he turned off the light and started down the road. *Nothing at all. You must have left the car door open or something. That's it. The door was open.*

But the door had not been open.

As Max drove home, he became increasingly aware that he was being watched. The road seemed darker than usual, and he could just barely see in front of him. His coworker lived closer to the country than he did, and only a few blinking street lights illuminated the area. Most of the houses were surrounded by small parks and green spaces.

There are lots of trees in this part of town, Max thought with a shudder, *and lots of animals in the trees.*

Suddenly, Max swerved his car and slammed on his brakes, screeching to a halt in the middle of the road. Something large was sitting just out of the aura of his headlights. It was crouching on its shaggy haunches, so still it looked like it was cut from stone. Max sat in his car breathing heavily. His hands were gripping the steering wheel so tightly his knuckles were white—it was all he could do to keep them from shaking. He could just barely make out the creature's eyes. They were inky black and reflected the glow from the car's headlights.

It blinked, then slowly walked off the road.

I'm drunk, Max thought as he sped down the street. *I had wine at the party. I'm seeing things. There was no creature. There is no fur in my backseat. I'm drunk. Nothing more. Nothing to fear.* But Max was afraid. He was more afraid than he had ever been in his life. Deep down, he knew he was sober. He knew that everything he saw was real. That's why he was driving as fast as he was able, hoping he could escape before the creature caught up to him.

When he pulled into his driveway, he ran into his house and locked the deadbolt on his front door. He locked his bedroom door too, just in case there was something in his house. He threw himself on his bed and covered his head with blankets. He tried to sleep, but each time his eyes closed he saw the large, hulking form sitting in the road, or Anna's rosy face smiling up at her father.

When he was finally able to fall asleep, he dreamed of a wolf sitting in a recliner and drinking beer, and of little Anna howling at the moon and asking to eat his heart. He couldn't be sure which one it was, for all the images morphed together.

* * *

"Did you sleep well last night, Max?" asked the secretary as Max punched his timecard the next morning. His usually well-oiled hair was somewhat messy, and his tie was knotted with less precision.

"Yes, pretty well" he responded, forcing a smile. "It was just—the storm last night kept me up. The wind kept howling by my window. Oh well!" Max forced another smile and walked away quickly. The secretary's pale red hair reminded him all too much of Anna's curls.

Forget about her, he told himself. *She was just a random little girl. You don't want a family. You don't want love. You don't love anybody. She's not your child. She's just a random little girl who doesn't even know you exist.*

Yes, that was all Anna was. Just another innocent child in a world full of evil and hate. Just another small soul who believed all was good and kind. A child whose heart was full of love and laughter, who's best friend was a stuffed rabbit. Just a little girl who loved to nestle herself into the soft curve of her mother's abdomen, pushing close to the little sibling she didn't yet know.

As Max made his way to his desk, the secretary looked at him out of the corner of her eye, puzzled at his odd behavior. "But there wasn't a storm last night," she tried to say as he left. "My dog always wakes me when there is a storm, and he was fast asleep." Max didn't hear her though, he was lost in his own thoughts.

Max sat down at his desk, *a very important desk*, he reminded himself, and began looking through a stack of paperwork his supervisor had placed there. He clicked his pen anxiously and tried to calm himself, but only managed to stare blankly at the papers in front of him. Five minutes passed and he still hadn't gotten anything accomplished. He clicked his pen again in agitation and finally stood up and made his way to the water cooler.

Carl was also getting a drink, and greeted Max with a somewhat sleepy, "Good morning." Max nodded at his coworker then quickly turned around without getting any water.

"You okay, Max?" Carl called out.

"I just need some air," Max squeaked, and nearly ran back to his desk, opening the window and leaning out till the breeze cooled his flaming cheeks. The strange gnawing feeling washed over him again, but this time Max understood—he was hollow inside.

He looked down at the people passing by on the pavement. Instead of eyeing them with a dim sort of superiority as he had yesterday, he looked down with a sudden envy of their lives.

A woman passed on the street with her arms full of packages. Who were they for? As Max caught a glimpse of her pleasant, smiling face, he knew she hadn't bought them for herself. Only he stood truly isolated, locked in a tower of his creation, only able to look despairingly out the window and wish to join in the steady throng of people walking below.

Max searched for the coveted treasure in the crowd, as if studying the people would help him find what his own life lacked. All the other employees had long since begun work and a few of them eyed Max uncomfortably as he absorbed himself in the grimy view out the window.

As Max scanned the city below him, an odd figure caught his eye. At first, he thought it was a dog, weaving in and out of the crowd. The large gray animal went unnoticed as it dove between a man's legs and scampered forward. Max couldn't believe his eyes. *Why doesn't someone try to catch it?* he thought. It must have gotten loose from its owner, or it might be a stray.

Suddenly, the animal stopped right underneath Max's office window. It looked up at him with a disquieting expression in its eyes, threw its head back, and howled. All the fear Max had felt the night before seemed to surge once more in front of him, threatening to drown him in its tide. He let out a shaky breath. The animal was not a dog, it was a wolf.

I know that wolf, he thought. Max felt his face flush with fear, which soon changed into red anger. "I know you!" he said under his breath. "You stole everything from me." He looked down angrily at the wild animal below, still unnoticed by any but him. "You stole everything, and now I'm going to get it back." The wolf only blinked at him with its small black eyes and continued down the street.

Max ran from his place at the window and out the office door. There were a few murmurs and quiet gasps from his coworkers as they saw him race past them, looking determined and frightening. Max raced to the elevator door, but it was taking too long. After a moment or two of waiting, he headed for the stairwell. The wolf might be gone by the time the elevator got there, and Max wouldn't let himself lose the wolf.

When he got to the street, the people hurrying around him felt overwhelming. From his office window, Max could watch them from an appropriate distance and muse about their lives, but on the pavement, he was just as much a pedestrian as they were. For a moment, he wondered if there was part of him still standing at the window, looking with displeasure upon himself.

Max shook his head. The wolf, he needed to find the wolf. Where was it? A quick scan and he saw that the creature was standing a little way off, staring directly at him. It was larger than he saw from the window, more the size of a small bear than a wolf.

"Out of my way!" called Max as he pushed through the crowd. He couldn't remember a time when he had been so outwardly rude. But he didn't care now.

The creature flashed a strangely human-like smile as it saw Max come charging towards it. It turned tail and ran, always staying just out of Max's reach. It was as if it were mocking him.

Not if— surely it was.

It ran across a busy street and slowed to see if Max would follow. He did and nearly got bumped by a taxi driver who shouted angrily from his cab. Max shouted back and kept running.

After a block or two, Max was holding his side as a sharp pain twisted through his insides, leaving him puffing and breathless. The wolf slowed too but seemed as persevering as ever. It darted into a dark alleyway and waited for him to follow.

"I've got you!" Max cried, diving into the ally after it. He was exhausted. The creature backed itself into a corner between a brick wall and a dumpster and faced him with an unholy expression. It was trying to look meek and frightened, and for a moment, Max bought it. He stepped closer, trying to catch his breath, and looked into its wet black eyes.

I will not tell you what Max saw in the eyes of the wolf. Only that it was then he realize it wasn't a wolf at all. It may have had claws, fur, and teeth, but that was just there to clothe something else, something old. It was a wolf in sheep's clothing, or rather, something in wolf's clothing.

"I want my heart back," Max demanded, his voice faltering slightly.

The wolf made a sound between a whine and a laugh. Then it spoke. It spoke just as it had when he was a boy.

"You can't get it back. It's mine." The creature stepped closer, side-eyeing him with those damp little eyes. "I own you."

An icy shudder rippled down Max's spine. "No, you don't," he said with a quiver in his voice. "You can't own me." He watched the creature in disbelief, open-mouthed and frightened. It took another step towards him. He could smell the boggy stench of its breath. "Hey! Get back!" Max yelled. He stomped his foot at the wolf like it was a stray dog. "You don't own me! You stole my heart! I was just a child!"

The wolf recoiled, then began to laugh. It smiled at Max, feigning kindness. But there was a smile under its smile if you understand me.

"A silly boy to a silly man. Why do you need a heart at all? You gave me your heart. I didn't steal anything."

It was then that Max knew why he couldn't love. Hatred And Bitterness had consumed his heart, and now, Hatred And Bitterness was inching closer to him.

"See," it said. "It was a fair deal we made. You're mine. All mine." The greed and hunger in its voice were sickening. Max stood there stupidly, hanging his head.

"And this time," it went on, "I'm going to eat all of you." With a jump, it lunged towards Max's throat.

A yell issued from Max as the creature knocked him down. He felt his head crack against the concrete, making sparks fly before his eyes. The thing was standing right on top of him, one oversized paw on his chest to hold him down. Max struggled to keep its over-eager jaws away from his face, holding back the toothy mouth that pushed towards him. His head ached from the fall, making him weaker than usual.

"Somebody help me!" he called. "Mad dog! Help!"

Nobody can help you now, dripped a voice in his mind. It was the same voice he heard at the dinner party, the voice of the wolf. *Nobody is coming to the rescue. You don't need anybody, remember? You don't need anyone and nobody needs you.*

"No!" Max yelled, trying to shove the thing off of his body. "Stop it! Give my heart back and leave me alone!"

Hot spittle fell on Max's face as the jaws inched ever so much closer to him. His strength was waning and the creature showed no signs of tiring. The saliva felt warm and sticky on his face and burned like vinegar to the skin.

What can I do? thought Max. *I'm going to die.*

He thought of Anna once again, sweet and innocent in her white nightgown. Surely there was no hatred inside of her.

With a sudden realization, Max yelled—"I forgive him!"

He felt the wolf falter and growl angrily. With an almost hysterical hope, Max repeated, "I forgive him! I forgive my father! I'm not angry at him anymore!"

The creature yelped in pain. Was it just him, or did the wolf feel lighter? Smaller, too?

"You can't forgive him!" it said in a half-broken howl. "How could you when he didn't ever love you?" Its voice dropped lower. "Your mother didn't love you either. You *have* to hate her. She left her own son."

A lump rose in Max's throat, but he swallowed hard to push it back. "I forgive her too!" he cried. "I forgive my mother for leaving. I forgive my father for not caring! I forgive them! I forgive, I forgive, I forgive."

The wolf howled and contorted into an unnatural shape. It reared onto its hind legs and tried to bite Max, but shrieked in pain and shriveled into dust. A foul odor was all that was left, and even that dissipated in the cool breeze.

The wolf was dead, but Max could only lay on his back and weep with relief, feeling his heart beat for the first time in twelve years.

THE LAKE

 dreamed again last night," Leanna said to her brother when he found her in the stable. She was grooming the big chestnut mare and sneaking her bits of apple from the kitchen. "I dreamed truly, but no one believes me." Leanna made a face. She was a strange girl, and nobody understood her. Her brother Thomas, however, remembered when they had both been children and seemed to see things the same way. Of course, he put childish thinking aside, but not so his sister. She was almost the age for marriage, but how could she make a proper wife when all she thought about were the brownies and sprites she swore lived in their croft?

Finding her with the horses was bad enough. Their father didn't approve of her going to the stable. According to him, she was too flighty to be trusted around the animals. It was really Thomas's job to look after the horses, but she always seemed to find herself there when she was upset.

Apparently she told their parents about her dream, but they had only laughed and told her not to think of such nonsense.

"What did you dream?" Thomas asked. He didn't know if he would believe her either, but she was, after all, his sister.

"I was in a white dress—" she started.

"You often wear white," he interjected, as if it discredited her dream. Leanna didn't seem to notice.

"My dress was billowing in the wind behind me like a bird," she went on. "I was in the forest all alone. It was dark, and it was night. Why was I outside at night?" she asked him.

"Who knows?" said Thomas with an indifferent shrug. "It was only a dream. I once had a dream that—"

"That's different," his sister said firmly. "Just listen. In my dream, the sky was as dark as pitch. There were no friendly stars, only a bright white moon on black velvet. The wind was howling like a wolf and I was scared.

"I started running, faster than I have ever run before—and I can run quite fast you know."

She waited until he had nodded his head in agreement before she continued.

"When I ran, I wasn't sure from what I ran. I just knew something was after me. I ran through the forest until I came to a pond that looked like black glass. I went right up to the water's edge and stared into it. My reflection stared back, and told me—"

"See," said Thomas. "Reflections don't talk. It was just a dream."

"Maybe your reflections don't talk," she snapped, annoyed at his interruptions. "Mine did. She mouthed that there was something in the water. I wanted to jump in and find what she spoke about. She said it was something precious, something valuable. But to think of that cold black water going over my head. Oh!" Here she shivered as if the cold already surrounded her.

"It was just a dream," Thomas said quickly. "It would be best to just forget about it."

She shrugged.

"You don't believe me either."

"Of course not," he said, and he didn't.

But her dream had certainly unsettled him. His sister had strange habits and never spoke with the other village girls. Sometimes, she would spend hours alone doing only Heaven knows what. Perhaps this was just another oddity of hers, but Thomas did not want to believe that she had dreamed truly.

The next morning, Leanna burned the eggs and accidentally gave her father a jug of clumpy cream with his porridge. Her eyes were bleary and her hair, which was usually tied back into two brown plaits, was messy and uncombed.

"Did you sleep well?" her mother asked.

Thomas had just slid into his seat at the table and was hastily gobbling his breakfast before going to the fields.

"No," said Leanna. "I dreamed truly last night."

Her mother clucked,

"You did nothing of the sort. See to your chores, girl, and no nonsense."

"What did you dream?" Thomas asked later that day, as he found his sister fixing the gate surrounding the hen house.

"The same thing I dreamed the night before," she said. "I was at the pond in my white dress and wanted nothing more than to jump into it. Something precious was underneath the surface. I needed it."

"It was nothing but a dream. You shouldn't worry about it," he said.

"I'm *not* worrying," she said, as she tied a post steady with some flax. "Why would I worry?"

"Exactly," he responded. "Dreams are just dreams. Nothing important happens while you sleep."

But Leanna went through her day as if in a daze, and the next day as well. This went on for some time, until at last her family became worried.

"There's something wrong with that girl," her mother would say, and shake her head.

"Aye," her father would return. "That there is."

But only Thomas asked about her dreams.

"When you dream," he asked. "What does the pond look like?"

"It looks like the pond half a mile from here," she answered. "You know, the one in the forest, by the foot of the mountain? The one we used to play by as children."

"Of course," he said. "How could I forget? But those days are behind us. I haven't played in the forest since I was a boy."

"Pity," she said, looking at him with an expression that made him squirm. "Then where do you play?"

"I don't play," he huffed.

Leanna's eyes were still bleary from the lack of sleep. *Or too much of it*, Thomas thought, and her hair was still unkempt. She began singing strange tunes as she worked, and constantly hummed a song that no one had heard before.

"How pretty," said her mother. "Did you make that up, Leanna?"

"I suppose so, Mother," said Leanna, blushing at the compliment. "I might have made it up, but in my true dream…"

"Not this again!" roared her father. "Leanna, listen to me. It ain't proper to carry on so. You're going mad, and I for one won't have it. A dream is a dream."

"Yes, Father," she said, and was silent.

She stopped speaking of her dreams after that, even when Thomas asked her about them. Instead, she would only look at him and bite her lip, her eyes brown and misty like lake water. She still sang her melody, though. Thomas could almost place where he had heard her song, almost, but not quite.

One morning she didn't come down to breakfast. Her mother looked worried and Thomas mirrored her sentiment.

"Is she ill?" he asked.

"She has never been ill a day in her life," said their mother. "But I should go check on her."

Thomas waited in the kitchen as their mother went upstairs to the girl's small bedroom. He heard her gasp, and he nearly flew up the stairs by her side. His sister was sitting up in bed and blinking at the cold sunlight filtering through her window. She was soaking wet as if she had plunged herself into a river, her long hair dripping and her white nightgown transparent with water.

"Where am I?" she asked. "Only a moment ago it was night."

"She's bewitched!" cried their mother. "Leanna, why are you all wet?"

"I haven't the faintest idea," she said. "I swear I have been in bed all night."

Their mother just shook her head. "Witchcraft," she murmured.

"I'm not a witch!" cried Leanna "I'm not mad either, or ill. It's just—" But she could find no explanation to what had happened. "I'm sorry, Mother. Whatever it is, it won't happen again."

But the next morning Thomas found her in the barn, crying.

"Brother," she said with a pale face. "It happened again. I woke up wet and shivering—and I dreamed truly!—I woke up right as I was about to find what I was searching for. The lake covered my head with water, but I was so close."

"Sister," Thomas said quite seriously. "Do not go into that pond again."

Leanna said nothing, but only turned and went inside the house.

That night as his sister slept, Thomas crept into her bedroom to keep watch. He watched and waited, hour after hour, until it was midnight, the time when Old Man Sleep crouches at bedroom doors and waits to grab people and take them to their dreams. He waited and watched, but he only ever saw his sister sleeping peacefully in the moonlight, her thin, strong hands folded underneath her sunny cheek, breathing deeply with sleep.

Bit by bit Thomas nodded off, only to wake with a start when it was morning, his sister sitting up in bed soaking wet and looking at him quizzically, wondering why he had slept on her floor.

The next night was the same. He watched, he waited, he woke with the dawn, but still his sister was soaking wet. This time she was trembling.

"I almost had it in my hands," she said, "but it sank too deep. All I saw was a glow of light reflecting on its face."

On the third night, Thomas made sure he would stay awake. He pinched himself, and paced about the floor. Whenever he felt his eyelids grow heavy, he would walk to the window and stare out at the waxing moon.

It was 3 o'clock when he heard a noise coming from his sister's lips. It was as soft as a breath, but his ears pricked at the sound. It sounded like a little laugh, merry, and delighted. Then he saw a silent shadow glide from his sister's form and slip out the window. He threw open the shutters, and popped his head out of the open lattice. There in the garden, he saw his sister silently sliding barefoot across the mossy lawn. He rubbed his eyes. His sister was still in bed, but somehow her dream self had stolen away towards the forest.

Quickly, Thomas pinned on a cloak and rushed outside after her.

"Leanna!" he called. "Leanna! Come back!"

But her dream self did not seem to understand or hear him. She only walked towards the forest with a smile on her face and her white nightgown flowing freely in the chilly wind. By the time they got into the woods, the wind was howling. Thomas caught her shoulder. "Sister, come home," he said.

Her dream started as if frightened and looked at him with terror. She turned quickly and began to run, the wind howling in the trees overhead as she went deeper into the forest. She didn't stop until she was on her knees and staring into the dark water of the lake. There were no stars above, only the moon, shining big and luminous in the sky. He could hear his sister singing to her reflection, and he finally remembered the song.

In our land of lake and bower
And tree to climb up like a tower
Where elves have hid their treasures old
For flowers bloom as made of gold

For truly, this was the place where they played as children. Thomas could see the hollow where he and his sister had crowned themselves king and queen of the woods, and the tree where they spent so many summer days eating berries and twisting gorse into wreaths. Yes, this was the spot where he had left his childhood.

Leanna stood up and began wading into the lake, her hair spreading out as the water went past her neck, making ripples in the moonlight.

"Come back!" Thomas cried. Who knew what was in that water? It certainly frightened him, and the thought of his little sister's head being covered by that cold blanket made him shudder. Thomas ran in after her, splashing into the pool, and caught the back of her skirt. "Come back! You'll drown!"

As he did so, his head went under water. Thomas tried to gain footing, but the fringe of his cloak caught on a submerged tree branch. It was then he realized how cold the water truly was. His fingers, grown clumsy without warmth, slipped as he tried to unclasp the pin holding his cloak around him. He struggled in the icy bath, frantically trying to free himself.

His reflection paled in the frigid water and seemed to glow with moonlight. Thomas felt his lungs quiver in his chest as the air left them in a sudden burst of coughing. He would have drowned, but a slim hand, grown strong with farm work, pulled him out of the water and dragged him onto the shore.

He coughed and sputtered on the rocky bank as his sister clung to him and cried as if her heart would break.

"I found it!" she sobbed. "I told you it was precious. I found what I was looking for."

And at once, they were back in Leanna's room. Cold, and sopping wet, but laughing in the morning light, with tears in their eyes and smiles on their lips. For it was only a dream, but they had dreamed truly.

MELODIES

The wind was restless that night. It seemed to tug, to pull, to whisper at you as you walked past.

A gentleman in a dark suit and slim leather shoes clutched his cap as the wind tried to knock it off. He gruffly muttered about the 'confounded weather' and continued on his way. A poor woman bustled out of a house and bobbed a small curtsy as he passed, only to have the wind pluck at her skirts and carry her shawl down the road. She chased after it, then hurried down the street to her destination.

All night the wind kept it up. It ran through the streets, blew leaves into the air, and rattled at the window frames. A child peeking out of an upstairs gable thought she saw the wind's face staring back at her. But she must have been dreaming; as soon as she blinked it was gone.

Outside the quaint little town, there stood a small house. The white picket fence surrounding its small garden was peeling from age, and weeds were sprouting between the cabbages. The wind placidly flicked a few more paint chips off as it hurried past. Then it leaped over the small gate and stomped through the unkempt vegetable garden.

Inside this house, in a small attic bedroom, a young woman sat with her head in her hands. She was crying. Crying because there was no time to paint the gate and no time to weed the garden. There was no time for anything. Her mother was sick and all she could do was wait and worry. She could hear her mother tossing uncomfortably in the bedroom below, shivering despite her burning fever.

The young woman slipped out of bed and dried her pale cheeks with the back of her hands. She crept down the stairs and began stoking the dying embers in the hearth, small bits of ash floating into the air. When the fire was blazing again, she sat back quietly on her heels.

She was looking at the family portrait sitting on the mantelpiece. It had been painted last summer by a traveling artist, and though it lacked detail, she and her mother treasured it. The painting depicted them arm in arm, wearing their best dresses and smiling joyfully. They had always been a small family, but they were happy. It scared the young woman to think she might lose her mother.

As she was thinking, her eyes lit upon a small instrument lying on the corner of the mantelpiece.

Mother's violin, she thought tenderly as she saw it. The young woman remembered all the times she had been sad as a child, and how her mother had played for her.

A muffled groan came from her mother's bedroom. The young woman glanced towards the door in concern and bit her lip. It had been a long, hard year for the both of them. Their familiar house seemed like such a strange place now without her mother's cheery smile. The young woman sniffed and reached towards the violin. Perhaps she would feel better if she tried to play something. A gust of wind blew down the chimney and tugged encouragingly at her hair.

She picked up the bow and rested her chin on the chinrest. The wind howled outside the house like it was cheering her on. The young woman didn't notice, but took a deep breath and began to play.

She started slowly at first, occasionally screeching through a note or two. She wasn't nearly as good as her mother was—or used to be before the sickness made holding the violin heavy and burdensome. Soon, a sweet melody was pouring out of the fiddle and filling the gloomy little house.

Across town, another musician was lying awake. The wind was keeping him from falling asleep and rattling his window so hard he thought it might break the glass. He was in town for only a short while, just to finish up business with the bank. He was a wealthy young man and had been working for his father's law firm ever since he turned seventeen. How was he to tell his father that he detested office work? He was only a clerk and errand man now, but someday—his father promised with a pat on the shoulder—someday, the whole business would be his. The thought made him twitch.

The young man got out of bed and reached for his flute. How was he to tell his father that he loved to create? To write music? To take raw sound and forge it through the furnace of his brain until it was poetry? The things he would have said if he only knew how!

Another violent rattle of his window broke through his thoughts. He sighed deeply and closed his eyes. He liked to play with his eyes closed, imagining that he was a famous musician in the largest concert hall in the world. He played softly at first, still conscious of the other travelers in the inn, but soon forgot about everything except his flute.

"Hey!" someone called out from the corridor. "I'm trying to sleep!"

But the young man paid no attention.

At the cottage, the young woman was still playing her mother's violin. The tune she carried was not one that she knew, but it felt right to play. The woman and the man played together, their melodies drifting through time and space. They were aware of nothing except the warmth of the melody and the longing they felt. The wind was the only one that heard their song. If only they knew, if only!

The wind threw itself against the lattice of their windows, trying to make them understand.

I'm so lonely, thought the girl as she played by the fire.

I'm so empty, thought the young man in the inn.

"Just step outside!" the wind seemed to say. "Just step outside and I will take you to a man who can help you. Just step outside and I will show you a girl you can love."

But of course, neither the young woman nor the man heard anything but a howl and moan from the wind.

The door to the young man's room opened, revealing a stern-looking innkeeper.

"Knock it off," she said sharply. "Do you think you're the only one in the whole house? Nobody can sleep with you making that racket. The wind's bad enough tonight."

The young woman's playing stopped abruptly as she heard her mother call for water. She carefully set her instrument down and ran to her mother's side.

"Did I wake you?" she asked softly as she held a glass to her mother's once-red lips. Her mother was beyond conversation, but she managed a shake of her head.

"Pretty," was the only thing she could say. The young woman's eyes filled with tears, and she nestled close to her ill mother.

Outside, the wind howled with frustration and shook the leaves from the trees.

~ PART TWO ~
THE FAILED HERO

It came like a shadow, the silver voice
Of despair with her chalice of pain
For who can resist her seductive glance
Or break her fettered chain?

But she cried aloud when she could not grasp
A boy who deified his shame
For when the sun shone on his flint-like eyes
It sparked them into flame

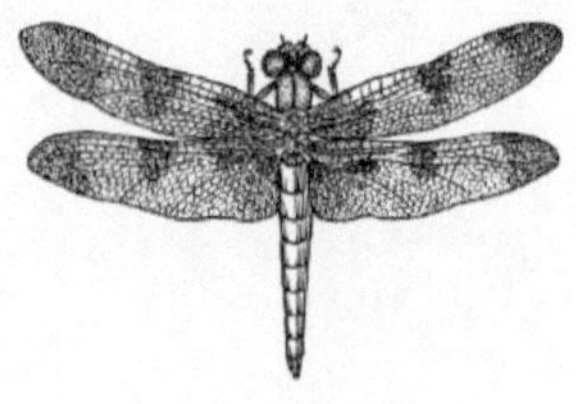

AUTHOR'S NOTE

I would not call this story a novel (it's much too short), but a short story doesn't sound quite right either, despite the title of this collection. Calling this a novelette might be more accurate, but in reality, this is a thought experiment in narrative form.

In every story with a hero, they are faced with an impossible task, and in every story the hero *almost* gives up in their darkest hour. But this seldom really happens in books and movies. Frodo didn't go back to the Shire when faced with Mount Doom, though he could barely crawl by the end. Odysseus escaped Calypso's island, and even Edmund found redemption. Victory is sweet and certain in worlds like these, but in our world each day is uncertain. It makes us beg the question: what if the hero failed? Would they mend their mistakes if they could, or would they tempt others to join in their unhappy company?

This 'experiment' is not meant to be a full storyline. When reading this book you are abruptly dropped inside two larger stories as they converge. Both characters are experiencing their ultimate low point, the "abyss" of the monomyth. One is acting as a sort of mentor to the other, although, by the end, you may change your mind about who is mentoring whom.

Again, this is a thought experiment, not a novel. Read it as such.

What the Storm Brought In

he sun rose fast and red like the fiery billows of a dragon's mouth; its coppery head climbed past the mountains' jagged peaks and dappled the forest floor with light. An old man, weather-beaten and hunched over with arthritis, was slowly limping towards his goat shed. The sun, though hot and angry in the sky, was filtered by the dense canopy of pine trees and shone a pale honey color on the man's face and hands. Each bulging vein and scar could be seen in the early morning sun. These were hands that had toiled many days and were hardened by work. Hands that had fought, and caressed the faces of those he used to love.

He opened the old barn door with a grunt and his two doe-goats rushed at him, bleating for food and vying for his attention. The man chuckled softly at the two brown-spotted animals butting against his legs. They had been his only companions for many long years, and their mothers before them. They were practically his children.

He locked the first goat into the milking stand and began rhythmically milking her. His life was simple. Wake at dawn, milk his goats, and work until sundown. It was all he could do to provide for himself so far away from other people.

The goat's milk was flowing rich and frothing into the bucket. The steady sound of the milk streams reminded the man of the soft sweeping of a broom and his world slowly fell away into that of early childhood.

"Mother, Mother! Eric says I can't play swords with him." The comforting face of his mother looked up from her sweeping and her eyes twinkled as she beheld her youngest son. *"Why not, Fynn?"*

"He says I'm too little." The boy's small lip puckered into a frown. "But I'm not. I want to go on a quest too. Look, I even have my own sword!" The snub-nosed boy held up a weapon made of two sticks crossed over and fastened with a blade of grass. His mother's face broke into a wide smile and two rosy apples filled in her cheeks.

"Well, brave knight. I have a task for you." The sweeping stopped, and she picked up a basket.

"Fill this with eggs from the chicken coop. If you do it fast, I'll give you a currant bun."

The boy eagerly grabbed the basket and swished his sword in his other hand.

"I'm not afraid."

The goat let out a bleat. The man had stopped milking and was now staring blankly at the dusty particles of hay floating in the barn. Tired of being trapped in the stand, the goat let out another bleat and kicked the bucket of milk onto the ground, spilling its contents on the floor. As if awoken from a dream, the man slowly righted the pail and put a calloused hand on the animal's back.

"Sorry, old girl," he murmured as he untied her head. "Some things are better left forgotten."

***

The whole day felt hot and expectant of a storm. The old man's eyes were ever turning skyward and watching the clouds as they scuttled and expanded in the sky. Bulging and twisting themselves into shapes before gusts of wind broke them apart. The man was sitting by the doorway of his hut and carving a block of wood into the shape of a bird. He was adding the minute details of feathers onto its face with a very sharp knife, carving the wood grain into something real and beautiful.

A gust of wind blew the wood shavings off the man's lap. The sky was darkening by the second into deeper and deeper hues of gray and the mountains in the distance looked smudged and watery, like ink bleeding into parchment. Another sharp gust brought the man inside the hut.

He set down his knife on a small table and then placed his carving on the mantelpiece above the fire.

He stared at the small wooden bird for a long time and heaved a heavy sigh.

"Fynn, do you see the birds?" a girl's voice drifted back to him. "Look how gentle they are, and how sweetly they sing."

Her voice broke and faded away into the crackling of the fireplace. The old man threw another log on the flame and turned his back from the hearth. *Forget it, old man,* he told himself.

The quiet pattering on the hut soon turned into a steady stream pouring down outside. The man hurried to close the shutters covering his glassless windows. His goats would be cozy enough in their snug hay-filled barn, but his own hut was full of leaks and cracks that the bitter north wind always found. His hut was the work of an unskilled man hastily building a dwelling before winter. The only weatherproof room was his own small bedroom which he had patched up long ago.

The man went around lighting candles and occasionally stoking the fire. He took a large cast-iron pot and hung it on a sturdy hook above the flame. He added milk, tubers, and wild plants then let it boil. Soon the hut was perfumed by the delicate scent of carrots and wild thyme. As his dinner was cooking, the man placed bowls and saucers where rain had found its way through the thatching of the roof and ran down the beams holding up the ceiling. It seemed the whole storm was trying to get in his hut, like the rain itself was seeking refuge from the gale.

The soup simmered on the fire and lightning thundered outside. The man filled a wooden bowl with the soup and seated himself on a three-legged stool near the table. The carrots and other roots swam in the broth as the man stared absentmindedly into his bowl. There was another storm like this where he used to live. But that was many years ago.

***

The man was awoken from sleep by frantic banging on his door. The night was thick and the rain was still pouring outside. He jumped from bed as quickly as his aching joints would allow and hobbled across the hut. He heard wheezing and coughing on the other side of the door. "Who is it?" he called, preparing himself for violence.

"Please…" the voice sounded feverish and desperate. "Help me… please."

The man's heart fluttered. "Friend or enemy?" he called out.

The voice was on the verge of tears. It tried to respond but could only utter a croak. It was taken by another fit of coughing before it could speak. "Friend."

The old man quickly undid the latch, the door creaking open as a youth stumbled through the doorway. The man caught him in his arms before he fell. He was breathing hard, and a shattered sword hung at his waist.

"Easy! Easy, you are safe here," said the old man as he held up the visitor.

"Heaven be praised," murmured the boy.

His light hair was matted and soaked with water, his cloak torn and stained with blood.

THE DAY BETWEEN

he old man passed the night on the hearthstone and the boy slept fitfully in the bedroom. Twice he called out in his sleep, and twice the old man strained his ear to hear the call. The cries were either in the boy's native tongue or utter nonsense, the old man could make nothing of it.

He looks young, the man mused as he lay by the crackling fire. *Too young for war. Why, he can't be more than seventeen.*

But what did he know of war and the world outside his hut? Times and customs change, and there is never a proper age for war. War kills old men and corrupts the young.

Yes, yes, he thought. *Times change. Besides, you were young yourself when—* But he cut himself off abruptly and pushed the thought aside.

He wore velvet on his cloak, and his belt looked of fine leather. There are no nobles here, though. Perhaps he is a thief and stole them from a king's son. Perhaps he is a scoundrel.

The old man was not frightened of thieves or robbers. He had nothing worth stealing. The old man chuckled to himself. *Unless a robber wanted the clothes off my back, I could give him nothing.* He scooted closer to the fire as a draft blew past him. The rest of the hut was hollow and cold and he felt the dampness in his bones. The youth coughed in the other room.

Poor lad. Even if he is a scoundrel he's near enough to death now.

What a change the storm had brought. It had been hot and humid just yesterday but overnight the rain turned the hut into a dismal and dark place. The storm had brought the boy too. That was sure to mean something.

"Storms always bring ill tidings," muttered the old man. "Cold and wind and bad news."

Mud streaked the floor where the youth's boots had dragged across the wood. *I'll have to clean that later*, thought the old man. He stood up with a grunt and shuffled to the door leading to his bedroom. He cracked it and peered into the small space. The boy lay on his back, fully clothed, on the man's bed. His skin was pale as the moonlight shining on it, and drops of sweat beaded on his brow. His breaths were so shallow that if it were not for the dull rasp he made the man would have thought him dead.

Tomorrow he will need a bath and fresh clothing, and a good hearty meal. Goat milk will do him good. Too bad I couldn't get off more than his boots. That scabbard looks like it's pinching him at every breath. Poor lad. Look what fate's done to him!

But the old man was no longer thinking about the boy. *Oh well. Let him sleep.*

The storm blew itself out and left a foggy haze in the morning sunlight. Branches and leaves blown by the wind scattered the forest soil like a carpet. The old man was busy with a mop and broom, trying to tidy up the mess from the night before. When he had set his hut in order, he went out to gather firewood, leaving the stranger alone.

The forest was wet with dew and mist. The old man had an ax on his shoulder and was inspecting trees in a nearby fir grove. He found a dying one and began chopping, the sound of his ax echoing into the distance.

Deer lived in this wood. Gentle, quiet creatures who liked to stay out of sight. Sometimes hunters would come from nearby villages to bring venison home, but they seldom killed more than a few. The deer were so elusive that they were nearly impossible to find. The old man respected their desire to stay out of sight. There were many days when he wished he could become one of them. But of course, he was a man and not a deer, and desiring something does not make it so.

The mist clung to the old man as he chopped and mixed with his sweat. By the time he had cut halfway through the tree, he was dripping with moisture. *You're getting old, Fynn, he told himself. This tree isn't even big.*

The tree started to lean to one side, and with a shove from the old man's leather boot, it crashed onto the dank floor. The old man sank down on its stump to rest, breathing harder than he thought was usual.

"I've never seen fog like this before," he said as he wiped his brow. "It's as white and thick as goose down. Doesn't look like it will lift today."

A bird trilled in the canopy overhead. The call sounded close to the man's left, but the bird was completely shrouded by the mist. The man whistled back before shouldering his ax. Then, rising on creaking knees, he set out for home.

He returned to the spot half an hour later with his goat pulling a cart. He chopped the fallen tree into small pieces and then loaded them up for firewood.

The rest of the day was uneventful, and the man slept on the hearth again that night.

THE YOUTH

he old man threw another log on the fire as a quivering voice came from the bedroom.

"Hello?" it croaked.

"Are you awake, friend?" called the man, standing up and moving to the room.

"Yes, Father, I am."

The youth was sitting up in bed as the old man entered. He was handsome, and had the cropped hair of a warrior. The boy's eyes were large and dark gray, uncommon in the old man's country. He noticed this right away, but said nothing.

"Do not try to tell me who you are," the old man cautioned. "You're weak, and speaking will tire you. I didn't think you would survive the night."

The boy coughed then winced from the motion. "I didn't think I would survive it either. My horse was killed and I've been forced to walk since then." Another fit of coughing took him and the old man hurried out of the room to get him water.

When the youth had drunk, he sighed deeply. "Is this house near Toke?" he asked.

"Yes, about a two day journey."

"Only two days more," murmured the boy, closing his eyes and resting his head on the pillow. "Two days more."

"Friend, can you stand? There is a stream nearby."

"Yes, yes I can stand. But I will need your help. Please help me."

The boy shifted into a seated position and the old man helped him up. The boy groaned as he stood.

"Heavens I'm stiff." His deathly pale face broke into a laugh. "I really got battered up."

He unclasped his belt and let the ruined sword clatter to the floor, then undid the cloak wrapped around him and let it fall near the sword. The cloak would have been beautiful, if not for its wear. It was embellished with the crest of a crimson stag, antlers raised in defiance. It was a rich man's cloak.

They were a slow procession going to the stream. Even if the youth had been strong, the mist from the storm obscured their view, making it hard to see the way.

The stream was still swelling from the rain, and now ran tumbling over the smooth stones on its bed, laughing at the buttercups that grew by its bank. The youth undressed and slid into the water, shivering as the cold surrounded him. His body was covered in cuts and scrapes from battle, and his back had the lashes of a whip.

"I left some soap near the bank, friend. It will help get the dried blood off." The old man moved downstream and began washing the youth's clothing, turning the water murky with grime.

I wonder who gave him those marks, and where he got his cloak. Perhaps he is not a criminal, perhaps he is a knight.

The man shook his head.

A hero.

He could hear the youth coughing and moving about in the water.

Well, he thought, *we'll have it out of him eventually. He's foreign, so perhaps he is a noble after all.*

"Do you live alone, Father, or is your wife away?" called the boy, nearly invisible in the fog. There was a slight twinge in his voice, as if calling out hurt him badly. It was well masked, however.

"Don't raise your voice," the old man called back, perceiving the boy's pain. "I will answer your questions when we get back to my home. But first we must get you clean and I must milk my goats."

When the youth finished washing the old man helped him from the water and gave him a rough blanket to cover his nakedness.

They traveled back to the hut and the man jerked his head towards the door.

"Wait in there by the fire and dry yourself. I need to take care of my animals."

The old man crossed the hut's threshold a few moments later with a pail of fresh milk in his hand. He found the boy huddled near the fire with the cloth wrapped tightly around him. He was murmuring something under his breath and rocking back and forth on his heels.

"Are you saying a spell?"

"No, Father. I don't believe in magic of that sort." The youth smiled wryly. "But I can't tell you what I said."

"Is it a secret?"

"Yes, Father."

"Do you harbor many secrets?"

"No," said the youth. Then he frowned as if he remembered something. "Just one, but that I cannot tell you." He said this fiercely, then bent his head and coughed.

"I'm sorry, boy, I won't ask again." The old man put the milk aside and took a sack of oats out of a wooden cupboard in the wall. He scooped some into a pot full of water and set it over the fire.

"You asked if I had a missus," he said conversationally. "I don't, I've been alone here for a while now."

The old man glanced at the youth when he didn't respond. He had slumped against the wall and was back at muttering. "But I was in love once."

The youth quieted and fiddled with the edge of the fabric. "Were you?"

"Yes, I was. Her name was Runa. She lived in my village." For a moment the old man's eyes brightened. "She could mend a bird's wing faster than lighting. She loved them."

"What happened?" pressed the boy, when the man's eyes lost their gleam.

"Nothing happened. I left her."

"Left the girl you loved? Who loved you?"

"Yes. I left and never came back, and there is no use in bringing up old memories." The old man pointed to his bedroom door. "I have an extra shift in there. I suggest you dress yourself before breakfast," he said curtly.

When the boy had dressed and seated himself at the table, the old man placed a bowl of porridge in front of him.

"Thank you, Father, and sorry." The boy looked down at the table's knotted wood sheepishly. "I had no intention of accusing you. Life has a way of going the opposite direction just when you think you're on the right path. I should know."

He said the last part quietly, but the old man's hearing was still keen and his eyes softened at the boy's comment.

"Forgive *me*, boy. I'm just an old man. I brought it up, you had all rights to be curious."

The youth took an uncertain bite of his food, then, seeing it was good, wolfed it down with great, ravenous bites.

"Do you not have porridge where you're from?" asked the old man.

The youth shook his head. "We do. It's just—I nearly forgot what food was like." His mouth was full and his slate eyes were as large as teacups. "It's been days."

"How long have you been on the road?"

"Since last spring, but that was centuries ago."

"And you are going to Toke?"

"Yes, Father," he said between bites.

"Am I right in thinking you are from Elden? A noble, too?"

The boy looked up from eating and gave the man a wry smile. "What tipped you off?"

"Your cloak, and your eyes. No one has dark eyes here. I suggest you hide your face when you enter Toke, lest someone try to stop you."

"I thought the lord of Toke always welcomed those from Elden." The boy frowned. "But it seems there are traitors all around us." His eyes went steely, and his jaw clenched.

"Peace, boy. The lord of Toke is a good man, but this land has been troubled by strangers, especially near the city. I don't know what your business is, but by your wounds I suspect you have made enemies."

The boy nodded then coughed loudly. He put his head in his hands and breathed deeply to clear the wheezing in his lungs. "Many enemies," he said, "like the sand on the shore. But this path was not my choice."

"That's a good thing. Count yourself lucky for that." The old man studied the youth carefully. "I have herbs to help with your cough, would you like me to make some tea?"

The youth nodded. "Please do. But I'm afraid it won't do any good. The cough isn't from sickness."

"Oh?" said the old man, raising his eyebrows. "What ails you?"

The boy grunted. "That's part of my secret."

SECRETS, OLD AND NEW

 *e's an odd one*, the man mused as he looked at the boy in front of him. *I wonder what his secret is. It presses on him like one of the mountains.*

"You should rest," said the old man. "Sickness or no, you're still weak. You must get on with your journey soon enough, and you're in no state to travel now."

"Do you think," questioned the youth, hopefully, "do you think I could start for Toke tomorrow?"

The old man looked surprised. "So soon? I would think you need a week at the very least. You were half dead yesterday…"

"No. No, I must leave as soon as I can, especially since I am to go on foot. I wish my horse hadn't died." The boy's face fell. "She was a sweet mare, spirited too. I broke her myself, but I should have taken one of the stallions. I never should have taken something I loved on a path so treacherous."

"Aye, lad, I know what you mean. My—" The old man cleared his throat, his eyes misty as an April morning. "I know what you mean. I will see about you getting on the road."

They sat in silence until the man said, "I have something I hope you will take with you. I've had it for a long time, but I think you need it more than I do. It's… it's a sword, from my younger days. It may help if you fall into trouble."

Now it was the boy's turn to look surprised. "Were you a soldier?"

"No, never a soldier. I never sought out war, but I sought something just as deadly—and more bewitching." The old man's eyes glowed with energy and youthful passion before he snuffed out the light. He looked embarrassed. "It is probably rusted, the sword I mean. But after a good polish it will serve you well. But the day is getting on, and I have work to do. You can find the sword underneath the bed."

He said this then left the hut rather quickly. He did not want the boy to ask questions.

How long will it take you, Fynn? How long will it take to forget? You senile old man! Do you still long for—

The last word excited the man more than he would admit. *—adventure?*

Outside, the morning sun was burning through the mist. The fresh smell of the pines contrasted with the damp smell of the wooden hut and the old man inhaled deeply as he stepped from his threshold. He swung open the twig gate surrounding his garden and headed towards a primitive tool shed. Really, it was nothing more than a few planks nailed together, but it kept the old man's tools from rusting and he was grateful for it.

He got out a spade and began to weed his garden. Weeds always sprouted fast after a heavy rain. He threw the plants spitefully into a pile, where by midday they would be nothing but leaves wilted by the sun. Seedlings were growing in the man's mind as well, the kind he too wished to rip out and throw away.

That poor lad, he thought. *It seems like all journeys are doomed to fail in the end.*

He looked at his withered old hands, all leather, and calluses, and spots. He traced the scar marring one of his wrists, faded almost to invisibility. He remembered when that wound had been raw and bleeding, and how he had hardly noticed the pain.

"Eric! Don't let go. Oh please… God, please…" The young man was crying hysterically. He had a busted lip and his hair was soaked with rain. Thunder boomed overhead.

"Stay calm, Fynn. It's okay. You'll be okay."

"No! No, don't say that. Just hold on a little longer!" The side of the ravine was slick with mud, nothing but a steep drop into the gully below. The rain had turned the whole valley into a river, rushing and swollen with water. The young man pulled hard on the rope, and then looped it around his wrist. He tried to pull his brother back onto the path, ignoring his purple hand when it went numb.

"It's not going to work. Just let me fall."

"Stop, Eric! Try to climb up. I'm not going to drop you!"

"I've tried, the rocks are too slick, I can only just hold on." His brother smiled up at him. How calm he looked! How happy, even! "Just let me fall."

The young man braced his back against a boulder.

"I said…" he grunted. "I said climb up!" The rope cut into his flesh, his blood staining the fibers red.

"It's never going to work, Fynn. It's okay." A knife flashed in his brother's hand. "I'm going to see Leah." His brother cut the rope knotted around his waist. "Save them for me, Fynn. Save them for me…"

When the sun reached its peak the old man was still kneeling in his garden bed. He could hear the youth limping over slowly, whistling a tune that was occasionally interrupted by a bout of coughing. He was still pale but his spirits were doing well.

"I've finished with the sword," the boy said, leaning heavily on the gate. "Do you have—Father, are you alright? You look white as a sheet."

"It's nothing. Nothing." The old man got up slowly, keeping his eyes on the ground to avoid the youth's gaze.

"Father?"

"I said I was fine," he grumbled. He pushed past the youth and began hobbling back to the house. He sat himself down on the doorstep and rubbed his face with his rough old hands, listening to the creak of the pine trees in the forest.

It was hot now that the sun was high, though a breeze was playing in the boughs. A woodpecker tapped away at a nearby tree, the whole wood sleepy and full with summer. There was something melancholy about the trees in this part of the wood. The oldest ones seemed to groan uncomfortably as the wind blew in their branches. Perhaps the trees wished they could uproot themselves and wander about the earth, building houses and cities as men do. Perhaps they, too, longed for adventure.

There's no reason to remember, the old man chided himself. The boy was still standing by the gate, looking at the old man with a disturbed expression. *Sorry, lad.*

"What did you say about the sword?" he asked, waving the youth over.

"I'm all finished getting the rust off. The blade is sharp as a razor." The boy forced a half smile and showed a cut on his open palm. "I learned that by accident. Do you have any oil or fat I can polish the blade with?"

The man nodded. "There's a pot of grease on the mantel."

When the youth returned, he held the sword and a rag dipped in tallow. He plopped himself down by the man and began rubbing the blade with smooth strokes. The old man could hear the boy's lungs rasping faintly with each breath, but thought it best not to mention it. The old man was still collecting himself and only stared at the ground. A beetle crawled in the dirt near the man's foot, its pronged feet making strange markings in the dust. He picked up the creature with his forefinger and thumb and absentmindedly inspected its shell as it tried to escape from his grasp.

"Tell me a story," asked the youth, abruptly. "Tell me about your life when you were young."

Still holding the wriggling beetle, the old man smiled wryly at the boy. The little black bug struggled between his fingers and flailed its hooked feet wildly in an attempt to get free.

"No," he said flatly, releasing the bug. "Memories are best left forgotten."

"Please?" pressed the boy, after a moment or two of silence went by. "It would help pass the time. Tell me about the girl you loved. I—" he paused, as if searching for the right words to say. "I too left someone dear to me, though not by choice."

"Who said I left by choice?" the old man said sharply. The youth looked surprised, then his face furrowed with curiosity. The old man sighed. *He's more persistent than a mosquito.*

"Well, Runa and I had been friends all our lives. We explored every inch of the forest, found every fox den, every bird's nest. She was a healer, an herbalist." The old man spat on the ground, annoyed at the irony.

"And?" pressed the boy.

"That's all I wish to tell," he grumbled, put out at the youth's nettling. "Now you must tell me about who you left behind."

The boy laughed, which degraded into a fit of coughing. "Her name is Clara. We met at the harvest festival."

"And?" the man pressed.

The youth grinned. "That is all I wish to tell."

THE OLD MAN

"Well," said the old man, rising despite his creaking joints. "I should get back to work."

"I would love to help you," said the youth, rising alongside him. "I've felt useless just sitting here and doing nothing."

"You're recovering from a brush with death," said the old man, "you should be resting, not doing farm work."

The youth laughed. "It's not in my nature to be idle. Besides, it's the least I can do for your kindness." The boy put on a brave face, smiling through his pain.

"Well, it would be nice to have help in the goat shed," the old man reluctantly admitted. "I can't exactly force you to rest. But bind your hand first. An infection is the last thing you need."

When they arrived at the barn, the goats were bleating loudly. As soon as the man let them out of their stalls, they immediately swarmed him, nuzzling in the folds of his clothes for treats.

"Easy, girls," chuckled the old man, running his calloused hand along their backs and fluffing up their fur in a way they loved. He turned to the youth and said, "There is a sack of salt in the corner of the room, get some for the animals."

The youth found the bag and grabbed a handful. His eyes widened with delight as the two goats licked the salt from his unbound hand, their pink tongues rasping at his palm.

"They remind me of my animals back at home," he said wistfully. "My father has a huge barn, plus a stable for the horses."

"Do you keep goats in Elden?" asked the old man.

"We have some," said the youth with a nod, "but cows are more common."

The old man shook his head. "Cows eat too much. Goats are a much better bargain."

The man propped open the barn door and turned his animals out, slapping them on the rump when they lingered by the door. Then he and the boy set to work cleaning the stalls.

After they swept the old straw and droppings from the dirt floor, the old man handed the youth two buckets.

"Fill these with water," he commanded. "If I don't rinse the milking stand, it will get too dirty to be near the milk." As the youth was leaving, the man called, "And make sure the goats haven't eaten my garden!"

The old man chuckled as the boy bowed deeply and left with the buckets swinging behind him.

* * *

It had been nearly half an hour since the boy set out to gather water when the old man began to worry. *The river isn't far*, he thought. *He couldn't possibly have gotten lost.* The old man swept some more goat droppings out of the barn. As he did, he looked into where the clearing met the forest, hoping to see a tall, lean figure coming his way. The old man frowned deeply when he saw nothing but the trunks of old pines, creaking as the mountain breeze blew against them.

Another woodpecker tapped away nearby. This time, it sounded like it was on the barn itself.

"Shoo, pesky bird!" the old man said as he went outside. He managed to frighten it away, and it flew into the forest, trilling shrilly as it went.

The old man sat down by the doorstep to wait for the youth to return. The woodpecker came back and began making another hole in the barn. The old man yelled and slammed his fist into the door frame, hoping to cause enough commotion to scare the pest. It left momentarily but came back again and again until the old man just let it be.

Tap, tap, tap, went the woodpecker. The old man put his head in his hands, trying to ignore the bird. *Just forget*, he told himself, *Just forget*.

Tap, tap, tap. The bird's drilling sounded like a frantic knocking on the side of the shed.

"Please stop," begged the old man, his face growing sadder by the second. The bird continued tapping. It really did sound like knocking.

"Let me in! Please, someone, open the door!"

The woman and young man jumped to their feet as someone banged on their door. The woman picked up her sewing scissors and motioned to her son.

"Open the door."

The young man sprang towards the entrance and flung it open, causing the visitor to nearly fall through the doorway, his face pale as death and hands shaking like an aspen leaf. It was storming outside. No one should have been visiting.

"Eric! What happened?" cried the young man.

"Fynn, Oh Fynn," the visitor's voice was shaky and masked with fear. He reached for his brother's face. He was sobbing uncontrollably. "It's come. It's already taken five people." Their mother gasped and ran to her sons, scissors clattering to the floor. "My wife is dead," cried the visitor. "The doctor could do nothing."

Finally, the bird flew away to its nest and left the old man crying in the doorway.

* * *

When the youth at last appeared by the forest's edge, his head was bent and the buckets hung heavy in his hands. The old man quickly dried his tears and hurried over to him.

"What happened?" he scolded. He wasn't really angry, but his fright and worry for the boy came out as annoyance. The boy shook his head and sat down to breathe, his lungs wheezing with every breath.

After a moment he said, "I'm sorry, Father. I… I guess I'm not as strong as I thought."

The youth was pale and sweaty, and though he hid his ailments well, the old man realized that he was much sicker than he let on. The youth was too exhausted to even ask why the old man had been weeping, for it showed readily on the man's face.

"Perhaps you should just get one bucket at a time," said the old man, his voice gentling as he looked at the boy. "Rest awhile."

The youth shook his head in disagreement, but when they reached the goat shed he sank gratefully onto a bale of hay.

"How am I going to get to Toke if I can't even carry water?" he said as he coughed into his arm.

"How indeed," said the old man, looking at the youth with concern. "How indeed."

The boy rested as the old man scrubbed the milking stand in the corner of the barn. They each drank some of the water left over from washing, and with some effort, wrangled the goats back into the shed, much to the sprightly animals' annoyance. The effort caused the youth to nearly double over with coughing. He assured the old man he was fine, but his youthful face looked pale and anxious.

After they finished in the barn, they walked back to the river to wash their faces in the chilly water. By the time they finally entered the hut, the sun was sinking like a doomed ship under the horizon, painting the sky's canvas in shades of red, gold, and purple as it drowned in a sea of stars.

What the Storm Brought Out

 t looks like rain again," said the youth that evening as he looked out the window. He was playing with a bug crawling on the window ledge and absently looking at the sky.

"Aye, that it does," said the old man as he put a bit of meat over the fire. Tonight, they were having rabbit, though the old man seldom had meat. He knew the boy needed more than wild vegetables and milk to get well, no matter how healthy he pretended to be. He'd been saving the coney for a week now, letting the meat age to perfection. He intended to smoke it so it would keep until winter, but now he was going to share his rations with the youth.

"You don't think it will keep me from starting out tomorrow, do you?"

"What was that?" asked the old man.

"The rain. It shouldn't hinder my journey, should it?" repeated the boy.

"No," said the old man with a frown. "No, I don't think it will."

Pity, he thought, *I hope the rain does keep him.* And with that, the old man silently prayed it would storm.

The youth turned from the graying night sky outside and sat down by the fire, meditatively looking into the flame. The old man was watching him out of the corner of his eye as he skewered their dinner onto a small metal spit. The boy's face was illuminated by the fire's blaze, making the shadows dance across him in the strangest ways. One moment, the light made him look like a child, the next, like an old man, full of ancient wrinkles and sagely spotted folds.

He seems happy, thought the old man as he watched. *He looks like I did when I was young, ambitious.*

With a sudden pang to his heart, the old man realized that he would never see the youth again. *He will leave me tomorrow. He will leave me and probably die on the road. The lad is too weak to travel all the way to Toke on foot. It would be useless anyway; he is bound to fail.*

The fire crackled in its place and mixed with the quiet pattering of rain outside. The youth coughed.

He can't even carry water. He's never going to make it.

For the first time, the old man saw the gaunt cheeks the youth concealed underneath his ready smile. The boy had let his facade slip for just a moment as he rested in the firelight, but the old man had seen all he needed.

Eric.

The old man remembered what his brother looked like all those long, hard months. How Eric had given his portion of food to him, and how bit by bit his brother wasted till he was nothing but spirit in bones. Of course, the old man grew thin as well, but not like his brother. Eric had sacrificed everything for him, and how was he repaid? With a failure. With a brother who could hardly save himself.

The old man squeezed his eyes tight. *Oh, Eric, I'm sorry, old chap. Please forgive me.*

He took one more glance at the youth sitting by the fire and made up his mind.

I can't let him end up like the rest of them did.

The old man broke the silence and said, "You could stay here, you know."

It took a second for the youth to understand. When he finally processed what the man said, his face fell. "What?"

"You could stay, you know. It's a quiet life here, but at least it's peaceful," repeated the old man. "You would never have to be on the road again." He shuffled up to the fire to roast the rabbit, looking away from the youth.

"Stay?" he heard the youth say. "No. I can't stay."

"But you're too weak to keep traveling," pressed the man. "If you leave now you'll never reach Toke. Two days of walking would kill you."

"So you suggest I give up?"

"I suggest you stay here." The old man dipped a spoon into a pot and ladled its contents onto the rabbit. "I don't hunt much, but you should be strong enough to trap game by autumn. I'm old. I'll need someone looking after things when I'm gone."

"Father, I wish I could…"

"—Whatever business you have in Toke can wait.

And it seems to me you may not be welcomed when you get there," he said, remembering the boy's wounds. Still, the youth refused.

"I can't. I have to get to Toke as fast as I'm able."

"But you'll fail," the old man whispered under his breath.

"What?"

"You'll fail," he said louder. "You'll fail because that's what all journeys are fated to do."

"Why would you say that?" the youth asked accusingly. His voice was steady, but the annoyance in his tone was unmistakable. The old man shrugged again.

"It's the truth. You would be better off if you stayed with me."

The youth did not respond, but his silence hurt the old man more than his words could. He heard the boy's breath gently rasping as he sat at the hearth corner. Rain pattered outside. The storm was blowing in.

The man sighed and turned to face the youth. He was looking despondently into the fire, not meeting the old man's eyes. He put his hand on the boy's shoulder.

"It's for your own good."

The boy's head snapped up. "I'm not going to stay. I can't. I already told you that." A cold fire flamed in his voice. He shook the man's hand from his shoulder and stood up. "I've come this far. I could never turn back now."

"But you can barely carry water! Do you think you would ever get to Toke on foot?"

The youth turned his back to the man and leaned his head against the wall, coughing violently as he did so. When his outburst subsided, he faced the man and once again showed that pale, gaunt look that reminded the old man of his brother.

"So that's what it is," said the youth. "Give up my quest. Forsake my friends." His speech was like a slap to the old man's conscience. "You don't understand what the stakes are for me."

"I can imagine what's at stake, boy," the man said firmly. "I've been through it too, but things don't work out like they do in legends. If there is one person you can save, it's yourself. You're bound to fail."

"Don't say that." The boy glowered at him. "If I stay, everyone I love may die. I may be weak but I'm leaving at first light tomorrow."

"It's useless, boy! I'm just trying to protect you!"

"Stop," commanded the youth.

The silence following pressed in; even the fire seemed to crackle a little quieter. The only noise was the rain outside and the wheezing of the boy's chest, sounding like the wind before a storm. He sat back down with his face turned away from the man, who paced pensively across the room.

"You just don't understand, do you, boy? You said it yourself, life twists just as you think you're going in the right direction. It's… it's like a cruel joke being played on us. We all think we're heroes, but we're not."

The storm outside began to roar and the shutters slammed against the windows violently, water spilling through the frame.

"I am not my own," rasped the boy, still sitting by the fire. A large, angry tear fell down his face.

"I'm the last person able to call for help. I have to try. You can't ask me to stay." He swallowed a lump in his throat. "I set out with four others, but men came in the night. They threw something strange into the fire. Our eyes smarted and we couldn't breath. I can't stay. You can't ask me to stay. How could you when they took... everything." The boy sat very still, his eyes glassy. "Everything..."

His shoulders shook. At first, it seemed as if he wept, but then the old man realized he was laughing. Not a kind, warm laugh, but the cold laugh of irony. "It's funny," the youth went on, shaking his head in disbelief. "The monks died blessing them, the very people that slit their throats. I just hope the Lord of Toke pities us enough to help."
Resting his head on his knees, he whispered an oath;

"I give my soul to protect my people
If my king calls I will come
If enemies attack I will fight
If the heavens rain fire I will not run
And like a stag, I will stare death in the face."

"Oh, lad! Oh lad, forgive me." The old man covered his face with his hands. "You have more heart than I ever did. You must leave tomorrow. I will not keep you any longer. I'm a ruined man. I thought that maybe I could save just one person. Maybe I could just save you."

The youth looked sadly into the fire, letting the heat evaporate his tears. "I am not to be kept as a pet. Saving me won't change what happened to you."

Aye, he is right about that, thought the old man. He made his way over to the fire and rested his head on the mantle above the flame.

"Well," he began, "I suppose it's only right if you know *my* secret." With a sigh, he went on. "There was a sickness in my village, a sickness with no cure. We heard rumors but didn't think much of them. But then people fell ill. It started with a rash, then a wasting consumed them. When the wasting came you could see it in their eyes. They looked so hollow." The man touched his own eyes with his fingertips, half expecting them to feel as sunken in with the horrors of his past. The youth's expression softened as the old man was forced to pause. "My brother's wife was one of the first to catch it. She—she was with child." The man's voice was shaky. "We couldn't do anything."

"How many died?" asked the youth, quietly. He was still staring at the fire but all the annoyance had gone from his face.

"Ten, before I set out, but they're all dead now. My mother, my friends, and Runa."

"Runa," whispered the youth. "That's why you left. You left to save her."

The old man nodded. "Her, my mother, and all of the rest of 'em. I asked her to come with me, but she refused. She said she needed to nurse the sick. She was a healer, you know, though it did little good in the end. My brother came with me. He put his heart and soul into the mission. We heard of new medicines in the west but…"

The youth looked him in the eyes. "But your brother died on the way, didn't he?"

The man's shoulders trembled. "I failed! I couldn't save Eric. Or Runa. Or my mother. I failed. I failed! I let them all down. Their blood is on my hands!

Oh, why did I live?" sobbed the old man. "Why, why must I go on? Why must I remember?"

The youth only wrapped his arms around the hunched old figure and cried alongside him. It was his first embrace in over half a century.

PATHS TO FOLLOW

efore dawn, the old man left the hut. The youth was sleeping soundly and never knew he left.

Through flickering lantern light, the old man found his way to his barn. He was carrying a burlap sack on his shoulder, a sack filled with all sorts of things. Wooden bowls, cups, leather scraps, trinkets, and extra clothes were all stuffed into the bag.

When he opened his barn door, his animals looked at him sleepily, confused at being woken so early. He hitched one of his goats up to his wagon and threw the sack in. He said nothing to his animals, though they looked at him questioningly with their large brown eyes. Instead, he only took a deep breath and led the goat to the woods, heading in the direction of the village.

When he came back, walking slowly into his clearing, his cart and goat were gone. In their place, a horse followed behind him. The man had traded almost all he had to get that horse.

Dawn came, and the youth woke. The old man was already cooking breakfast in the kitchen, and he set a steaming plate of quail and goat cheese in front of him as he sat down at the table. They were both somber with the boy's leaving, but determined that nothing should prevent him.

"Where is your stool, Father?" asked the youth as the old man seated himself on the corner of the table.

The old man shrugged. "I sold it."

"When?"

"Early."

The youth looked confused. "Why?"

"I will show you after breakfast. Eat all you can, you will need your strength."

The old man served helping after helping to the boy, until the youth finally resisted and swore he couldn't eat another bite. Still, the old man made him drink a large mugful of milk before he was really satisfied.

"Alright," the old man said when he was finished stuffing the boy. "Follow me."

The horse was chewing placidly on a bag of oats when they entered the barn, its head tied with a thick rope to the milking stand. The remaining goat bleated pitifully from the other end of the building, wondering where her companion had gone.

The youth stared in awe at the horse.

"How did you…"

"Oh, it was nothing," said the old man, feeding his doe a handful of grain apologetically. "I just traded some odds and ends for her this morning. The village isn't more than a few miles away. She's just a nag, but she'll get you to Toke."

"I know my horses, Father. This mare is not a nag." The boy gently stroked the horse on its muzzle. "She's beautiful. Look at that white star on her forehead! Her hocks are black, too. Has she ridden before?" he asked, turning from the animal.

"Yes, according to the man that sold her to me. I don't have a saddle, though."

"That's okay, I can ride without one."

The horse, curious of her new owner, began rubbing her head on the boy, getting bits of spittle and hair on his tunic. He coughed, then laughed aloud.

"I have a feeling we are going to be friends," he said, patting her lovingly on the head. "Starlight. That's what I will call you, Starlight."

He looks just like a true hero, standing there next to his steed, thought the old man, shaking his head in wonder. *A true hero. Just like the legends.*

"I'll be right back," he said, his eyes getting misty.

The old man hurried back to the hut. He had bought yet another gift for the boy. Simple though it was, the old man hoped to replace some of what he had lost. When he returned, he carried the polished sword and a brand-new cloak.

"Here," said the old man, handing it to the youth. "It's nothing compared to your old one, but the fabric is thick and warm. I tried to salvage your old clothes, but they nearly fell apart in my hands."

The youth smiled warmly. "You've done more than enough for me."

They led the horse out of the barn where it shook its mane in the crisp air. The boy untied the rope around its neck and re-positioned it to make a bridle.

"So you're leaving," said the old man. The youth standing before him was like the mirror image of his childhood self. He felt like he was telling his past goodbye.

"Yes," the youth said sadly. "I'm leaving."

"Don't forget me," pleaded the old man.

The youth paused tying the horse's bridle. "I could never forget you, Father. You saved my life. Without you, my country wouldn't have a chance." After a moment of silence the boy spoke again. "Maybe that was your quest," he said, his brow creasing in thought. "Maybe your quest was to help save my home, not your own."

He turned around to face the old man, eyes bright and shining. "Even if I never reach Toke, perhaps another will be helped by my defeat. Maybe everything stacks on top of each other and mixes together! Perhaps none of this is meaningless!

Father, what if you didn't fail? What if you completed the task set out for you?"

The old man was speechless. "And what is everything moving towards?" he finally asked "What will happen at the end of time?"

The boy's face glowed. "Something wonderful, I'm sure of it. When time stops, even death will bow to something greater!"

Could it truly be? wondered the old man. *It sounds too much like a legend, though I want it to be true.*

"Goodbye now," he said to the boy, patting him on the shoulder.

"Goodbye, Father."

With a smile, the youth cleared his throat and mounted his horse. Sunlight shone into his deep gray eyes and twinkled like firelight on a hot ember. As the boy turned, the old man watched the rider disappear into the distance, becoming nothing but a spec on the horizon.

Sunlight danced in the shadowy boughs of the pines, and a breeze drifted along, carrying the scent of wildflowers. It was a peaceful morning, the kind of day that makes one feel like the world was just born.

A large tear rolled down the bridge of the old man's nose. "May your path be level and always before you," he whispered. "God be with you, my son."

The End

ABOUT THE AUTHOR

Lilah Lyons is a Catholic writer from the United States. Since she was a child, she has longed for empty and wild places. When she is not writing, she can be found studying nature or eating blackberries. She hopes to fill her writings with Truth, Beauty, and Goodness.